For
*Tubby-toes, Hawthorn and Pteddy*
who all like picnics

*The artist would like to thank*
*The Bethnal Green Museum of Childhood,*
*Arundel Toy and Military Museum*
*and the Bear Museum, Petersfield*
*for the inspiration for many of the*
*bears portrayed in this book.*

First published 1987 by
Blackie and Son Ltd.
This edition 1989

Text of the Song 'The Teddy Bears' Picnic'
Copyright (c) 1932 B. Feldman and Co. Ltd.
London WC2H OLD

Reproduced by permission of EMI Music Publishing Ltd.
and International Music Publications

British Library Cataloguing in Publication Data
Kennedy, Jimmy
    The teddy bears' picnic
    I. Title   II. Theobalds, Prue
    823'.914(J)     PZ7
    ISBN 0 216 92661 0

Blackie and Son Ltd
7 Leicester Place, London WC2H 7BP

Printed in Hong Kong

# The Teddy Bears' Picnic

*Pictures by*
**Prue Theobalds**

*Words by*
**Jimmy Kennedy**

Blackie
London

If you go down in the woods today
You're sure of a big surprise.

If you go down in the woods today
You'd better go in disguise;

For ev'ry Bear that ever there was
Will gather there for certain, because
Today's the day the Teddy Bears
Have their picnic.

Ev'ry Teddy Bear who's been good
Is sure of a treat today.

There's lots of marvellous
Things to eat,

And wonderful games to play.

Beneath the trees where nobody sees
They'll hide and seek as long
As they please,
'Cause that's the way the Teddy Bears
Have their picnic.

If you go down in the woods today
You'd better not go alone.

It's lovely down in the woods today
But safer to stay at home.

# For ev'ry Bear that ever there was

Will gather there for certain, because
Today's the day the Teddy Bears have
Their picnic.

Picnic time for Teddy Bears,

The little Teddy Bears are having
A lovely time today.
Watch them, catch them unawares
And see them picnic on their holiday.

See them gaily gad about,
They love to play and shout;
They never have any care;

At six o'clock their Mummies
And Daddies
Will take them home to bed,
Because they're tired little
Teddy Bears.